For my east coast and west coast family.

Soli Deo Gloria

—N. T. L.

To my grandmother, who loves to hide fresh jasmine petals *under my pillow.*

—A. C.

Library of Congress Cataloging-in-Publication Data:

Tupper Ling, Nancy, author.
Double happiness / by Nancy Tupper Ling ; illustrations by Alina Chau.
pages cm
Summary: Told in verse, a Chinese American girl and her little brother protest the idea of moving, until their grandmother teaches them a special trick to make the change easier.
ISBN 978-1-4521-2918-1 (alk. paper)
1. Moving, Household—Juvenile fiction. 2. Chinese American children—Juvenile fiction. 3. Grandmothers—Juvenile fiction. 4. Stories in rhyme. [1. Stories in rhyme. 2. Moving, Household—Fiction. 3. Chinese Americans—Fiction. 4. Grandmothers—Fiction.] I. Chau, Alina, illustrator. II. Title.

PZ8.3.T8265Do 2015
[E]—dc23

2013039301

Manufactured in China.

MIX
Paper from responsible sources
FSC www.fsc.org FSC™ C104723

Design by Lisa Schneller.
Typeset in Kleide.
The illustrations in this book were rendered in watercolor.

10 9 8 7 6 5 4 3 2 1

Chronicle Books LLC
680 Second Street
San Francisco, California 94107
www.chroniclekids.com

Double Happiness

囍

by Nancy Tupper Ling • illustrated by Alina Chau

chronicle books · san francisco

The Move

I won't go!
I won't move
away
from our city house
by the trolley tracks,
away
from Nai Nai,
Auntie Su,
and Uncle Woo.
Today
we fly away—
and I don't want to go!

火车

Train

In my new room
I want
bunk beds,
fluffy rugs,
rocket ships
that **zoom**
and **zip**
across my walls,
a shark tank,
a fire pole,
a telescope,
and
no! Wait!
maybe . . .
just one long train
that rocks and wobbles
my bed each night.
I can't fall asleep
until the train passes by.

祖母

Grandmother

When I was young,
I placed memories
inside a special box.
It was my happiness box.
Always, it was near me.
Together you can make
double happiness.
Here's my gift to you—
a box of your own,
so happiness will stay close
no matter where you go.

Find four treasures each,
leading from this home
to your new.

熊猫

Panda

Nai Nai's panda sits
by the window
like always.
"I'll miss you," I say.
Nai Nai leans over me.
She places Panda
inside my box.
"He has a new home
now."

再见
Goodbye

A big squeeze
from Uncle Woo.

A smushy kiss
from Auntie Su.

"Don't you like to fly, Gracie?"
"No, not so far away."

宝藏
Treasure

I want things
that *grrrrrr*
and whirl—
greasy wheels,
paper planes,
copters, and toads.

Look, I'm a dragon now,
with sharp claws
and shiny scales.
I keep my dragon eyes
wide open for stuff
along the way.

幸运

Lucky

A rattle, a bump,
a glide, a roll—
this bus ride sure is fun.
Hey, wait,
what's under my
shoe—
dragon finds treasure!
It's old,
not shiny,
but **this** penny's
mine, all mine.

叶子

Leaf

One stray leaf
flutters down
onto my box—
Eucalyptus!
If I had a koala I'd feed
her this minty meal all
day long—
the perfect treasure
to remind me of home.

机场

Airport

Hip, Hop.
Wait here.
Hop, Hip.
Wait there.
Long lines.

People shuffle.
Sweaters and shoes.
Belts and watches.
We run to our gate,
then wait some more.

I ♥ San Franc
B

宁静

Quiet

I jump. I shout.
"Dragon needs more treasure!"
"Stop pouting, Jake."

"One penny,
that's all I've got."
"Keep looking, Jake."

"No fair.
You're always faster.
You're always better."
"Oh, brother!"

“**Huff puff. Puff huff.**”

Dragon blows fire.

Dragon stomps his feet.

“**Ssshhh,** you’ll wake Daddy.”

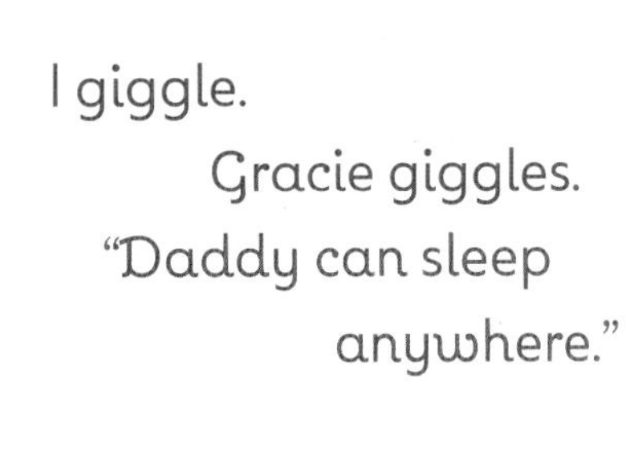

I giggle.

Gracie giggles.

“Daddy can sleep anywhere.”

蛇

Snakey

Ah-ha!
I found some gum
in my backpack.
I stretch it
and roll it
and ooze it
into one slinky snake.

Sssssee, his penny pillow.
Sssssee, he's *kai xin*—
so happy—in his brown box.
I'm tied with Gracie now—
two treasures each.

翅膀

Wings

The pilot lets me see
lots of whirly swirly
lights and buttons.
He gives me a high five
and a pair of wings.

Gracie pins hers on her shirt.
I tuck mine next to Snakey;
he needs wings to fly.
He is going far away.

图画

Picture

When we take off
I draw today:
our house,
my city,
the stinky bus,
Jake and me,
Princess the cat,
then Nai Nai waving,
the golden bridge
beside her.

I place the picture
inside my box
so I won't forget
these things
even if my new home
isn't **so** bad.

睡觉

Nap

"I'm not napping."
"Me, neither."

"Something sounds
like a tiger sleeping,
but I'm not sleepy."
"Me, neither."

I curl under the blanket . . .

"Snakey looks tired."

"Not me."

"Me, neither."

Zzzzzz

这里

Here

Brrr,
I wake to see
snowy streets
and icy cars
far below.
I wonder:
can I find our house
from the sky?

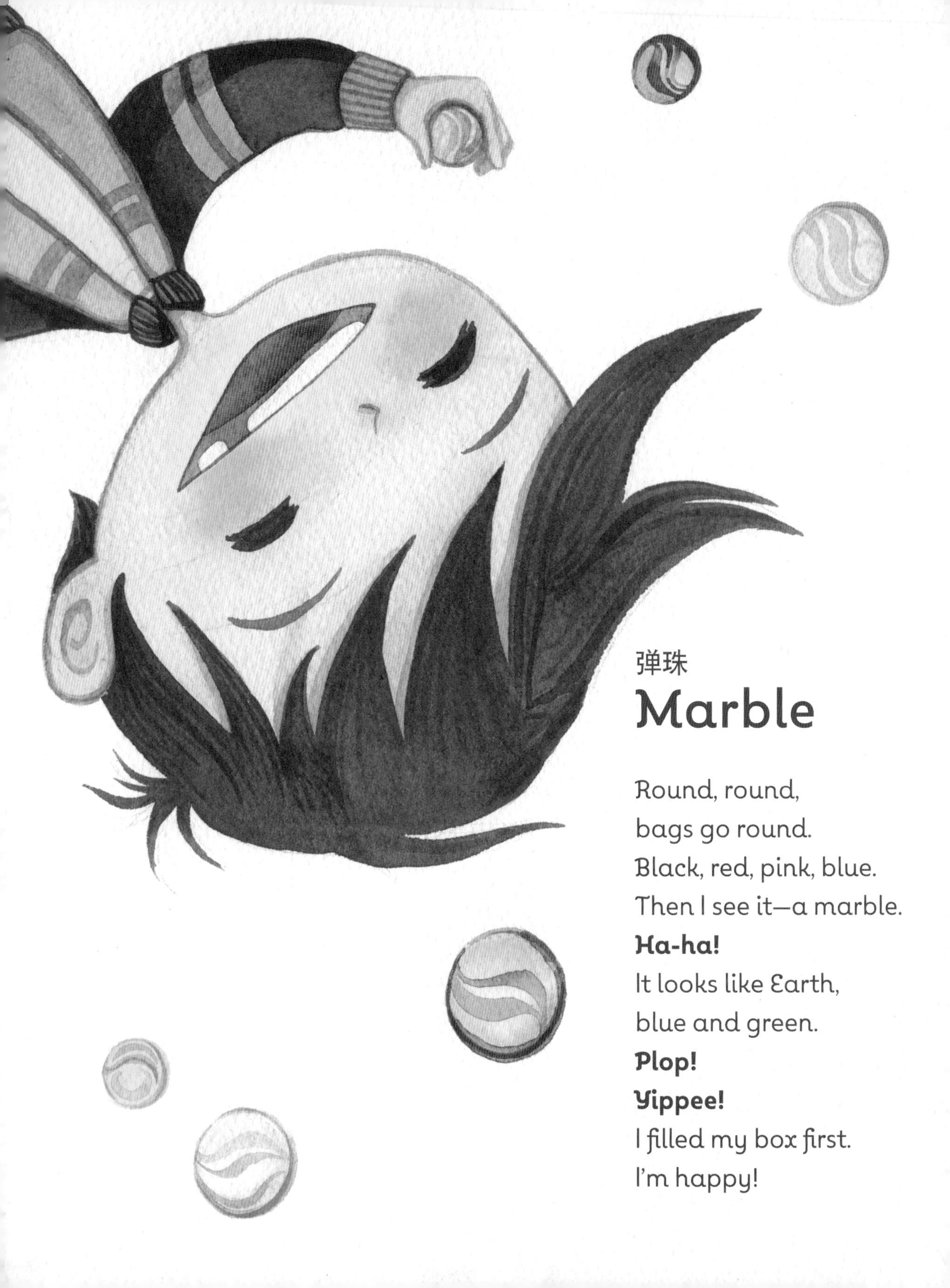

弹珠
Marble

Round, round,
bags go round.
Black, red, pink, blue.
Then I see it—a marble.
Ha-ha!
It looks like Earth,
blue and green.
Plop!
Yippee!
I filled my box first.
I'm happy!

伤心

Sadness

It's cold here.
I zip up my jacket.
People rush by.
Daddy stacks our bags
high on the cart.
I search for treasure.
"Time to go!" Mama says.
Lucky Jake!
Nothing reminds me
of home.
Nothing makes me smile.

家

Home

Yippee, windy roads

and piles of snow
lots of trees

and piles of snow
our big yellow taxi
makes a path

over lots of snow
up, up,
the curvy driveway

to our new home—
Hurrah!

探索

Explore

I won't like it here—
really.
There's no Nai Nai,
no Auntie Su
and Uncle Woo,
no city bus
or skyscrapers.
Wait,
what's that sound?
A train!
I hear a train.
Someone's happy.

房间

My Room

I race to the top of the stairs.
My new room:
it's bright, so bright and
stars light the ceiling.
"Hmm," I say to Panda.

"Maybe you'll like this room . . .
maybe? See the mountains!"
I count my treasures:
yi, er, san . . .
I still need one more.

晚餐
Dinner

Soon, the kitchen's sizzling.
"*Chi fan,*" Mama calls.
Come eat!
"Wait!" I say.
Something's missing.
I dig and dig
in a box marked PHOTOS.

"Here they are," I say.
I place the picture on the table.
Everyone's waving—
Nai Nai, Uncle Woo, and Auntie Su.
"Want to see our treasures?" I ask.
Jake and I hold up our boxes,
pretend they can peer inside.

惊喜

A Surprise

After dinner
I trudge up the stairs.
"I've got stuff for your box!"
I sigh.
"Thanks, anyway," I say.
It's pajama time.
I pop open my suitcase.
There,
on top of all my clothes,
the phoenix and dragon
stare back at me.

Nai Nai's silk scarf—
packed just for me!
I can smell jasmine
all around me—
just like home.
"Done!" Jake says.

"Ba," I say.
Lucky Number 8.

绘画

Paints

Before bed
we paint our boxes.

Mine looks like this:
three green loops,
a swishy tail—
Dragon watches
his train go by.

And mine:
a boy, a girl,
walking in the snow,
each with a box full of memories
tucked under their arms.

They look very,
very
happy.